Police Work

Written by Jill Eggleton

Illustrated by Jim Storey

Rigby

UNDERCOVER POLICE NEEDED

The Police Department needs more Undercover Police.

If you are interested in this work, please fill in the application form. Tell us about your experiences and why you would like to become an undercover police person. Please give a description of yourself, including: appearance, health, hobbies, and anything you may be afraid of.

APPLICATION FORMS are available from your local police station.
Please reply by August 12 to:

INSPECTOR LARSON
THISTLEDOWN POLICE STATION
45 THISTLEDOWN ROAD, RAGWORT
FAX. 555-4903

THE AD

3

Name: Millicent Froggit
Address: 2 Drain Rd., Wetlands
Phone: 555-6782
Age: 23

CONFIDENTIAL
POLICE CHIEF ONLY

Experiences:

I am an actress. I would like to work as an undercover police person because I think my acting skills would be useful. I have acted for people in many strange and unusual places. I have acted for divers on the seabed. I have even acted for astronauts in space.

Character Profile:

I am tall and thin with long, frizzy hair. I was born with hair the color of burnt toast, but I like to change it now and then. At the moment my hair is orange with black stripes – like a tiger's tail. I have long legs and I can run fast. People say I am as fast as a hare, so my nickname is Hare. I wear large glasses with purple frames. I like to wear different coloured socks and shoes. I don't like clothes that match.

My hobby is collecting goldfish. I have bowls of goldfish in every room of my house. Goldfish make me feel calm and relaxed after a hard day's work. I am a happy person and I love to make people laugh. I am afraid of one thing – toads!

Applicant #1: Millicent Froggit. Age: 23

Name: *Arthur Green*
Address: *41 Marks Rd., Newtown*
Phone: *555-3980*
Age: *51*

CONFIDENTIAL
POLICE CHIEF ONLY

Experiences:

I have been an accountant for thirty years and I know a lot about numbers. I can add a row of numbers at one glance. I would like to work as an undercover police person because I think the work would be an interesting change.

Character Profile:

I am not tall but I am as strong as a steel pipe. I have a round, chubby face and a big smile. I have no hair except for some fluffy tufts behind my ears. My eyesight is not perfect but I can see most things when I am close to them. Sometimes I use a magnifying glass when I am working with small numbers. I am very healthy except for the itchy bumps on my toes in winter.

My hobby is collecting rocks. I have a collection of rocks from all over the world. I am the treasurer of the rock collectors' club. I like doing crossword puzzles and playing chess. I think it is important to keep my brain ticking.

I am honest and reliable and a very hard worker. I am only afraid of mice and anyone who might steal my rock collection.

Applicant # 2: Arthur Green. Age: 51

Name: Luke Larsen
Address: 8 Browns Rd., Colville
Phone: 555-9234
Age: 19

Experiences:

I am a student at the university, studying photography. I have taken photographs in very interesting places. I have been high up in the mountains taking photographs of vampire bats.
I would like to be an undercover police person because I know the things I have learned in my photography work would be very useful.

Character Profile:

I am tall, with muscles as big as coconuts. I have short, black hair. I try to make it straight with hair gel. I am in good health and have excellent eyesight. My eyesight is so good, I can see a fly's eye without a microscope. I wear sunglasses most of the time because I like the way the world looks through them.

My hobbies are music and football. I have been the captain of the Colville's football team for three years. I play drums and trombone and belong to a band. In my spare time I play the trombone on the street corner or entertain the old people.
I am a caring person. I don't like to see people or animals hurt. I am only afraid of tornadoes. I think tornadoes are scary.

Applicant # 3: Luke Larsen. Age: 19

APPLICATION FORM FOR UNDERCOVER POLICE JOBS

Name: Sylvia McDonald
Address: 56 Smith Street, Snowden
Phone: 555-7327
Age: 28

CONFIDENTIAL
POLICE CHIEF ONLY

Experiences:

I am a deep-sea diver and I have been diving in many parts of the world. I have explored ancient shipwrecks and have been diving in waters thick with barracudas and white sharks. As a diver I have learned to be very alert. I think this would help me as an undercover police person.

Character Profile:

I am average height with long, stringy red hair that looks like spaghetti. I am very fit. I exercise at the gym and run ten miles every day. I can lift heavy weights and wrestle like a brown bear. In my work as a deep-sea diver I have to be strong. I have been wrapped in an octopus' tentacles and dragged along the seabed in the jaws of a white shark. Because of my strength, I have been able to wrestle free. My health is excellent. I only have a scar on my arm where I was slashed by the teeth of a barracuda.

My hobby is parachuting. I love leaping from a plane, feeling the wind on my face like needles of ice. I am a person who likes excitement. I like to have new and interesting adventures. I am not really afraid of anything, except having nothing to do and nowhere to go.

Applicant # 4: Sylvia McDonald. Age: 28

Name: Joe Monks (Frog)
Address: 2 Fells Rd., Carter
Phone: 555-5231
Age: 22

Experiences:

I am a crocodile hunter. I am good at catching crocodiles that have crawled into unwanted places. I once had to catch a crocodile that wandered into a tunnel. It was a challenge, as the tunnel was dark and narrow. I had to tape its jaws shut and take it back to the river. I would like to work as an undercover police person because I think the job would be similar to what I already do.

Character Profile

I am very thin and strong. People say I am as thin as a drinking straw. My hair sticks out like the prickles on a cactus. I can jump extremely high and I have won pole-vaulting competitions. Being a good jumper has helped me in my job. I have had to pole-vault over rivers full of crocodiles. That's how I got the nickname, Frog. My health is very good. I have never had the measles, mumps, or chicken pox. I do, however, have a scar on my leg where a crocodile clamped its teeth.

My hobby is cooking. I invent my own dishes using unusual ingredients. I am a person who likes adventure and I never like to give up. I am not afraid of anything much except my great aunt. I am sometimes afraid of her.

Applicant # 5: Joe Monks (Frog). Age: 22

Name: Fernella Sanderson
Address: 96 Trimble Ave., Trent
Phone: 555-9842
Age: 61

CONFIDENTIAL
POLICE CHIEF ONLY

Experiences:

I am a retired scientist and I have been all over the world studying fossils. I have studied the fossils of woolly mammoths, dinosaurs, and dodo birds. I would like to work as an undercover police person because I am too young to retire and I have many skills that would be perfect for this work.

Character Profile:

I have wiry black hair that is hard to brush. I don't like to look neat and tidy. I like to wear clothes that are different and outrageous. Sometimes I wear fur coats and hats with feathers. Sometimes I dress in a leather suit. Sometimes I wear flimsy clothes that flap around me like a flag on a pole. I have excellent eyesight. My ears are good, too. I can hear spiders spinning webs.

My hobby is motorcycle racing. I love to make wheels spin and dirt fly. In the rest of my spare time I like to gaze at stars and planets. I am very bossy but I think the job as an undercover police person would suit a bossy person like me. I am not afraid of anything. I AM FAR TOO OLD TO BE AFRAID OF ANYTHING.

Applicant # 6: Fernella Sanderson. Age: 61

17

DESCRIPTIONS

Descriptions are like talking pictures. The descriptions in this book are character descriptions. Each description "draws" pictures of the characters you met throughout the book.

How to Write Character Descriptions

Step One: Think about a character and the important things you want to tell the reader about him or her. Make a word web to help.

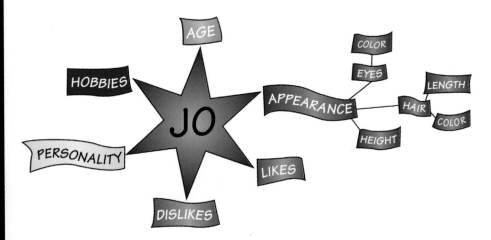

Step Two: Look at the word web and decide what things you will write about first, next, last.

1: APPEARANCE
2: PERSONALITY
. . . .

Step Three: Now use the word web to write a description. Use interesting adjectives.

I am tall and thin with long, frizzy hair. I was born with hair the color of burnt toast....

I am a caring person. I don't like to see people or animals hurt.

Use similes and metaphors to paint pictures in the mind for the reader.

Strong as a steel pipe.   Muscles as big as coconuts.

Thin as a drinking straw.

Step Four: Check your description.
Can you add anything to it?
Can you take out anything
that is not important?
Is your description like a talking picture?

Remember:
You can write descriptions about events, places, things...

Guide Notes

Title: **Police Work**
Stage: Fluency (4)

Text Form: Description – Character
Approach: Guided Reading
Processes: Thinking Critically, Exploring Language, Processing Information
Written and Visual Focus: Application Forms

THINKING CRITICALLY
(sample questions)
- Why do you think it is important to include things such as health, hobbies, and fears on an application form for undercover police?
- What else might be important to find out about a person wanting to be an undercover police person?
- Which characters would you choose to be undercover police people? Why?
- What skills do you think would be best for an undercover police person to have? Why?

EXPLORING LANGUAGE

Terminology
Spread, author, illustrator, credits, imprint information, ISBN number

Vocabulary
Clarify: application, confidential, undercover, treasurer, tufts, alert, flimsy, fossils, infested, outrageous
Adjectives: *long, frizzy* hair, *round, chubby* face, *itchy* bumps
Homonyms: tail/tale, hair/hare
Antonym: relaxed/tense
Synonym: ancient/old
Abbreviations: fax (facsimile), e-mail (electronic mail)
Similes: thin *as a drinking straw, as strong as a steel pipe, as big as coconuts,* wrestle *like a brown bear,* wind *like needles of ice*

Print Conventions
Colon, dash, apostrophe – possessive (collectors' club, fly's eye)